Tunnel Rescue

Stories linking with the History National Curriculum Key Stage 2

First published in 1999 by Franklin Watts
96 Leonard Street, London EC2A 4XD

Editor: Sarah Snashall
Designer: Jason Anscomb
Consultant: Dr Anne Millard, BA Hons, Dip Ed, PhD

A CIP catalogue record for this book is available from the British Library.

ISBN 0 7496 3353 0 (hbk)
0 7496 3537 1 (pbk)

Dewey Classification 941.081

Printed in Great Britain

Tunnel Rescue

by Dennis Hamley
Illustrations by George Buchanan

W
FRANKLIN WATTS
NEW YORK • LONDON • SYDNEY

LOND
SWINDON
READING
BATH
BRISTOL
BOX

1

It will never be done

Lizzie lived in a village a few miles east of Bath, with her mother, father, little brother Tom and the lodger Paddy, a navvy from Ireland. The year was 1837 and the young Queen Victoria was on the throne.

Pa and Paddy were arguing about the

railways as usual. A great iron road was being built out of London. Another was coming up from Bristol. On them ran great fire-breathing monsters which Lizzie could not even imagine. One day the two iron roads would join up and the village would never be the same again.

"So they say," Lizzie's father said. "The day it happens the world's going to end. Stands to reason."

"Why, pa?" Lizzie asked.

"Because squire and parson think so as well as common labouring folk like me. And that Mr Brunel – how dare he drive those smoking great things through hills that haven't been disturbed since Adam and Eve? That's what parson says."

"Then your parson's wrong," said Paddy. "Mr Brunel will drive his tunnel through the hills at Box and you'll all marvel at it."

Pa snorted and left for the alehouse. Paddy shouted after him. "You wait and see. Mr Brunel knows what he's doing." Then he left to go on the night shift in the tunnel.

* * * *

Lizzie was ten and Tom was seven. Already, railways were beginning to snake their ways across the land. But none of them was like the Great Western from London to Bristol that was being built by Isambard Kingdom Brunel. For a start, the rails were wider apart than usual. So the trains were bigger, faster and more comfortable.

Over the whole of Britain, navvies were living and working, digging cuttings, building embankments, laying rails – with

no tools but spades and pickaxes. It was the biggest change in the countryside since William the Conqueror came.

But from London to Bristol through the Box Tunnel, two deep miles through clay and solid rock? "It will never be finished," Pa said to Paddy.

Paddy had lodged with them since the railway was started. He was like a big brother to Lizzie and Tom. Especially to Tom. Often, after Paddy had finished his sleep after the night shift, the two of them walked over the hills and through the fields. Paddy talked about Ireland and taught Tom songs of home. "The Fields of Athenry" was their favourite.

Ma and Pa liked Paddy as well – and Pa would never *really* be angry with him. It was just his joke. But when Paddy came back to the cottage after every shift nearly dead with exhaustion, deafened by the sound of gunpowder blasting away the rock, Lizzie knew this tunnel was no joke.

2

Mr Brunel

One fine day in June 1839, Tom said to Lizzie, "Can we go and see Paddy making the railway?"

Two miles was a long way for Tom's short legs. When they reached the tunnel mouth, he was tired already. But the sight

they saw made then very quiet.

From the tunnel mouth at one end, horses pulled a never-ending stream of carts loaded with broken rocks dislodged by the gunpowder. It seemed as if the hill's heart was being torn out. As they watched and listened, they could hear the muffled explosions inside the tunnel.

Tom looked round. "Where's Paddy?"

"Paddy's inside the hill where the

gunpowder is," Lizzie replied.

"In the dark?" asked Tom.

Lizzie nodded.

They walked higher, away from the tunnel mouth and further up the hill. Here, a fresh breeze blew, sheep grazed the short turf and it was difficult to believe what was going on so far underneath.

But they could not forget for long. Soon they came to the first of the deep shafts sunk into the hill to let air in to the tunnel and to get the spoil out.

At the top of the shaft, a horse plodded

round in a circle, working a windlass from which a rope which stretched down, like the head of a huge well.

At the end of the rope was a big spoil bucket and more broken rock came up in it from the bottom of the shaft. Yes, and men went down and came up in the bucket as well – and sometimes, Paddy once told them, Mr Brunel himself.

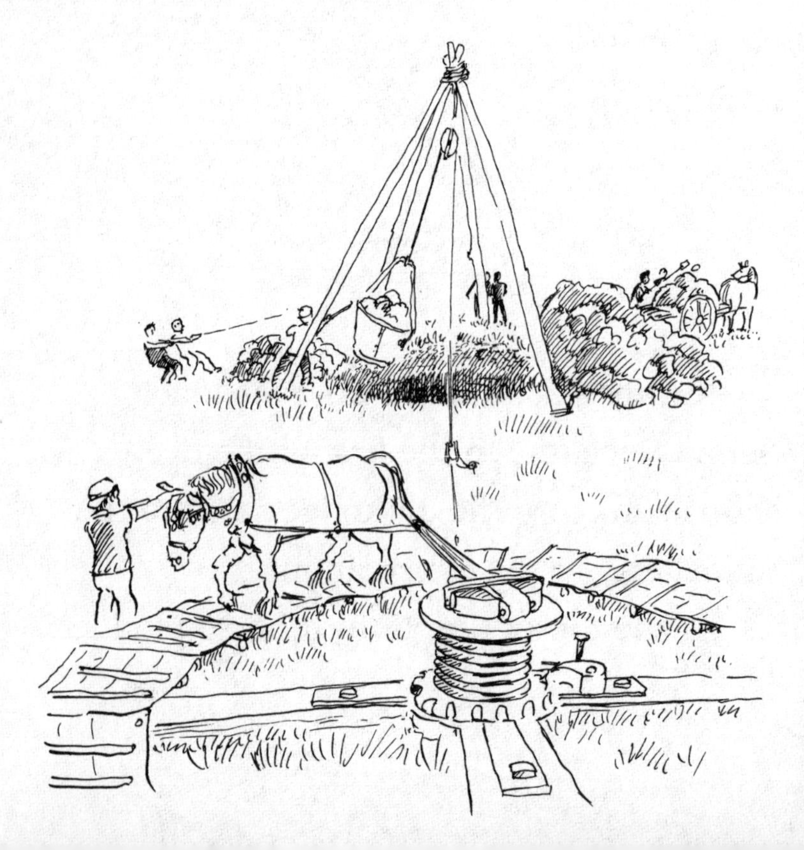

Going home seemed much further than coming there. Lizzie was wondering how much further she could go on in the heat and dust when Tom said,
"See what's coming."

A long black carriage pulled by four horses was beating along the high road.

"Get off the road, Tom," said Lizzie.

But as it drew near, she saw a man lean out and speak to the coachman, who pulled back the reins and shouted "Whoa!"

The carriage stopped and the man leant down to speak to them.

"Where are you bound for?" he called.

"The next village," Lizzie answered.

"That's two miles yet. It's hot and you deserve some comfort. Jump in and I'll take you there."

The inside of the carriage was dark and gloomy and smelt of cigar smoke. Plans, books and a tall stove-pipe hat were stacked on a shelf. A seat was pulled out to form a long couch. Lizzie at once knew where they were.

"This is the Flying Hearse," she said. "You're Mr Brunel!"

The man was small and wore a black coat. Lizzie liked his smile.

"And what do you know about the Flying Hearse?" he said.

"It's your coach," Lizzie replied. "You had it made specially so you could travel where you liked while you were building your railway."

"But tell me, girl," said Mr Brunel,

"What do they think about the railway in your village?"

"Well, they know it comes nearer every day," said Lizzie. "But my father, the squire and parson, they still don't think you'll ever do it."

"Why ever not, child?" said Mr Brunel.

"It's that tunnel. They say you can't make a hole through a hill that far and that deep without it falling in. Men are getting killed making it and so would passengers in the trains going through it. People aren't supposed to go under the ground until they're dead. God doesn't want tunnels in the ground. That's what the parson says."

"As to men getting killed," said Mr Brunel, "That I can't deny. Rocks and earth can fall, and floods can rise, and nobody can stop them but God Himself. But the navvies are good workers and brave fellows who believe in what they're doing. As to the other – well, if I tell you that too many people talk nonsense about the railways, what would you say to that?"

"I don't want our Paddy to get killed," said Lizzie.

"I'm going to drive trains through the tunnel when I'm big," said Tom.

Mr Brunel smiled and ruffled Tom's tangled brown hair. "And I'll make sure you do. Give me your names so I won't forget."

"I'm Tom. And this is Lizzie."

"Well, Lizzie and Tom, you speak a lot more sense than most of your elders. I won't forget you. And don't worry, your Paddy will come to no harm while I'm in charge."

The coach put them down by the village church.

"We'll meet again, Lizzie and Tom," said Mr Brunel. Then he nodded to the coachman and the Flying Hearse clattered on its way.

3

Floods

1839 passed and January 1840 came in with snow, frost and bitter cold. Paddy came home from his shifts shivering, wet and worn out. Things were not going well in the tunnel. February brought rain and the water pierced the rocks of the hill. By day and night two pumping engines worked steadily away keeping the tunnel dry.

Then one morning, Paddy never came home from his night shift. Lizzie and her mother waited an hour, then they went outside to find out what had happened. Only now were returning navvies trudging down the street, weary and drenched. Paddy was not among them.

"Floods in the tunnel," a navvy told

them. “The weight of water seeping through the rock is too much. It’s happened before. The pumps can’t cope.”

“Where’s Paddy?” Lizzie gasped.

“There are scores of men still down there,” was the answer. “And some will never come up again, I reckon.”

More navvies came. Still no Paddy. Lizzie and her mother turned back home. But then there was another noise. Horses galloped up the street. Yes – there was Flying Hearse heading towards the tunnel. Mr Brunel would not leave his navvies to struggle alone.

★ ★ ★ ★

Tom was very quiet when they told him. At last he said, "Mr Brunel said Paddy wouldn't come to harm while he was in charge."

"And he won't," said Lizzie. "Mr Brunel means it. He's gone to help."

"Why don't we go to help?"

"Because it's raining. We're not navvies. We couldn't do anything."

"Mr Brunel isn't a navvy, but he's doing something."

"That's different." She went back into the scullery to scrub turnips for their supper. She didn't hear Tom say, "No it's not." But she did hear the door latch close. She never hesitated.

"Mother, Tom's gone running off and I think I know where. I'm going after him." She snatched a shawl, threw it over her head and dashed out into the driving rain and sharp wind.

Lizzie ran along through the street, on to the high road – and there she saw him, the little figure struggling manfully on against the weather.

She had to run hard to catch him.

"Tom," she shouted when she was close. "This is silly. Come back home."

She grabbed him by the shoulders and tried to stop him. But he kicked out at her and shouted, "I'm going to help Paddy."

It was no use. She would never get him to come back. She would have to go with him and see he came to no harm.

4

The spoil bucket

They reached the cutting where the tunnel mouth disappeared into the hill. Already the water was pouring out like a river. Men and horses were nowhere to be seen. Lizzie imagined them all swept away in the torrent. So did Tom. “Paddy’s drowned!" he cried.

Lizzie stared at the grey, cold water. Tom must be right. Tears began to sting her eyes. Then she said, "No, why should he be? Mr Brunel's not here. So he's gone to the shaft. That's where the men will be rescued."

They pushed their way onwards against the wind blowing in from the Atlantic, up the slope to the top of the hill. All the while they could hear the beat of the pumps underground, as if the hill had two separate hearts, steadily pumping water out. Two carts passed them, pulled by horses, with weary, drenched men sitting, shivering.

"Men brought out of the tunnel," said Lizzie. Paddy was not one of them.

Now they found the navvies, flocking round the top of the shaft. There was Mr Brunel's Flying Hearse with the horses standing patiently. And over the heads of the navvies they saw a tall hat moving to and fro, as if its wearer was never still, never content merely to watch.

"He's there," said Lizzie.

"They won't let us get near," said Tom.

The windlass creaked as the horse

slowly moved in its circle. "The bucket's coming up," said Lizzie. Suddenly, everybody there gasped and moved over to the side of the shaft. The spoil bucket had come to the surface.

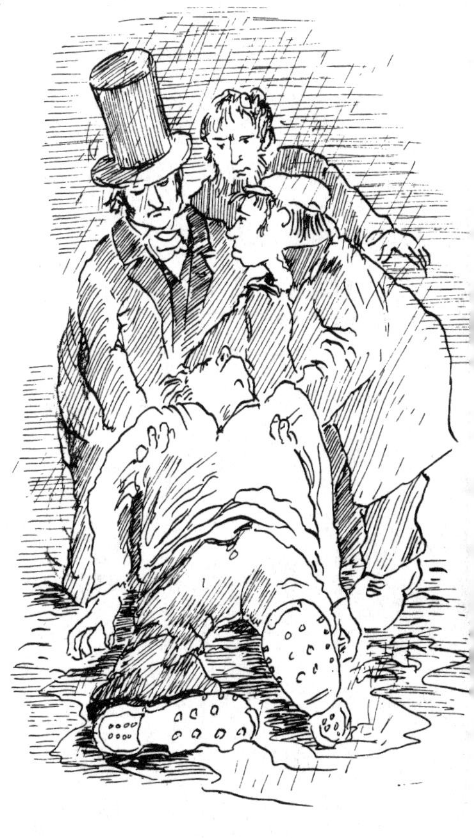

The rope was pulled over to one side and now the bucket was on the ground. Willing hands reached down into it. Three men were pulled out. They were limp, like rag dolls. Paddy wasn't one of them. The men were laid on the ground. Mr Brunel and the navvies bent over them. The spoil bucket, huge, rusty, mud-stained and wet, lay unattended by the side of the shaft.

Lizzie was feeling silly and helpless, but Tom wasn't. Saying, "I'm going to find Paddy," he ran away from her to the bucket, jumped, clung hold of its rim and then pulled himself over. She heard the thud as he landed on its iron floor.

Lizzie was horrified. She had to get in there herself and try to make him come out. So she too pulled herself up the side of the bucket and clambered over to drop into its dark smelly depths, up to her ankles in mud and freezing water.

By now she was furious with him. "What do you think you're doing, Tom? You'll get us both killed."

"I want to rescue Paddy," Tom answered stubbornly.

Suddenly there were voices very close.

"That's Mr Brunel talking," Tom whispered.

"And what's he going to say when he finds us in here?"

Before Tom could think of an answer, someone new climbed into the bucket. A navvy. He landed with his back to them and leaned out over the side again. "Give me your hand, sir," he said.

"Thank you, Smithson," said that voice they knew. And soon, the shiny boots and black trousers of Mr Brunel disappeared into the mud and water at the bottom of the bucket.

To their amazement, neither man had seen them in the darkness. Lizzie knew she should say something but her tongue seemed frozen to the roof of her mouth.

Lizzie felt the bucket lurch and sway sickeningly as it was pushed off the ground to hang suspended in the air above the shaft. She felt horribly afraid.

Then came the creak and squeak of the rope uncoiling as they were let slowly down. She felt Tom's hand searching for hers and then gripping it. She squeezed his in answer. But neither made a sound. Lizzie saw above them the circle of light which marked the shaft's lip grow smaller and smaller, further and further away, and the straining rope, seemed to stretch up into nothing.

And still they hadn't been noticed.

Now the darkness grew. The bucket swayed from side to side. Sometimes they hit up against earth, then, as they came lower, rock. By now it was pitch dark, except for the weak glow of the navvy and Mr Brunel's candles.

A bitter smell grew stronger. Water, earth and something else. It took her some time to realise what that something else was – she had smelt it on Paddy when he had come home and he had told her. It was spent gunpowder.

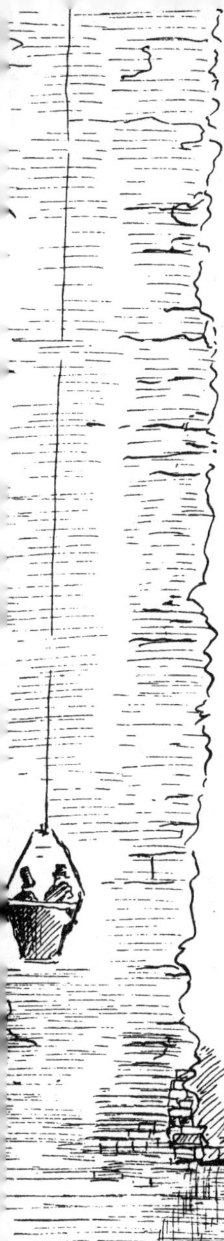

Now she could hear the sound of the pumps very loud indeed, wheezing, coughing, like old men about to give out completely. She heard the rush and flow and suck of water, more and more clearly as they descended. She remembered the parson saying from his pulpit at morning service: "No man should lie under the ground until he is buried by such as me." And she thought, *Parson's right. This railway and the tunnel should never be built. And Tom and me,*

we've come down here to die. We'll never see the daylight again.

The bucket landed with a slight bump as they reached the rough tunnel floor. Water was pouring past to a depth of about two feet.

"The level has fallen. We can walk along," said Mr Brunel. "The pumps are doing their work well."

It was at that moment that the two men moved. The navvy's boot trod on Tom's ankle. He yelped with pain. Mr Brunel and the navvy bent down with their candles to look closer.

"Well, now, Smithson," said Mr Brunel. "What have we here?"

5

Where's Paddy?

"You little wretches," Smithson roared. "Playing your games while good men may be dying. I've a good mind to . . . "

"Wait a moment, Smithson. Don't be so hasty," said Mr Brunel. "I know these two. It's Tom and Lizzie, if I'm not mistaken in this dreadful light."

"Yes, sir," whispered Lizzie. She was frozen with fright. So, by now, was Tom. He pulled at her sleeve, "Lizzie, I wish we hadn't come after all."

"Stand up," said Mr Brunel. They did so, trembling with both cold and fright. "And I suppose you've come to look for your friend," he said.

"Yes, sir," Lizzie mumbled. What dreadful punishment would he give them?

But there was to be no punishment. "Well, you shall," he said. "And before the evening's out we may be very glad of your services." He

turned to Smithson. "These children have one great advantage over us," he said. "They know exactly whom they are looking for. We should be grateful they are here."

He scrambled out of the bucket and they heard his feet splash into the water. Smithson followed. Then the two men leaned over and pulled Lizzie and Tom out. Smithson produced two new candles and lit then from the others.

"One of humanity's greatest needs," said Mr Brunel, "is for a source of bright, steady light which won't keep going out. If I live long enough, I must invent one."

The water came up over Lizzie's knees.

It was bitterly cold and she felt the hems of her dress and petticoat heavy and dragging underneath it.

By the light of her candle, she could see the walls of the tunnel, here rough and unlined because they had been blasted through solid rock. This truly was an awesome place. But she was determined not to die down here.

"What is your friend's name?" asked Mr Brunel.

"Paddy," Lizzie answered. "Paddy Egan."

"I don't know him, sir," said Smithson. "He wasn't on my gang."

"So where might we find him?" said Mr Brunel. "Do we look to the west or the east?"

Lizzie was silent. She could not answer and she felt ashamed. The two men

looked at her. She must say something.

"If it's any use," she said, "he smelt of gunpowder when he came off his shifts."

"Then east it is," said Mr Brunel.

"There's no point, sir," said Smithson. "We've got everybody from that end out who might be alive."

"You haven't got Paddy," cried Lizzie. "I *know* he's not dead."

"Then we'll look," said Mr Brunel.

They picked their way onwards, through freezing rushing water. They had to tread carefully, for large lumps of rock could be hidden under the surface. Many times they stumbled. The dim, flickering light of the candles showed the rock of the tunnel walls trenched with deep shadows where the gunpowder had blasted it out unevenly. The air was thick and hard to breathe: the sharp odour of gunpowder was strong and to Lizzie it seemed as though she was tasting rather than smelling it.

They heard a weak cry, "Over here." A navvy half crouched, half-lay in the water at the angle of wall and floor. They bent to him. His face was creased with pain. "My leg, I can't walk," he said.

It was not Paddy.

Smithson bent to him and hoisted him to his feet.

"Put your weight on your good leg and I'll get you back to the spoil bucket," he said. "We'll soon have you back in God's fresh air."

"Is there anyone else down here?" asked Mr Brunel.

"Have you seen Paddy?" Tom burst out.

"The young Irish lad? The last I saw, he was right up where the last blastings were made, as close to the rock fall as he could be, gouging out rock when the water came. I've not seen him since." The navvy winced with pain.

"I'll get you back," said Smithson. "I reckon there's no hope for your Paddy."

The two disappeared into the darkness. Mr Brunel turned to follow.

"Come on," he said. "You heard Smithson."

Lizzie and Tom stubbornly stood where they were.

"I'm going to find Paddy," said Tom.

"Mr Smithson's wrong," said Lizzie.

Mr Brunel bent down with his lantern and looked hard

in their faces.

"You're brave and loyal children," he said. "You deserve my help."

"How much further do we have to go?" asked Lizzie.

"I should say another hundred paces," said Mr Brunel. "Are you game for it? I've no doubt you can look after yourselves."

Tom never answered, but walked on through the water.

The way was becoming more and more difficult. Loose rocks were everywhere. Lizzie and Tom were holding their candles high and calling. "Paddy! Paddy!" Their cries echoed unanswered down the tunnel.

A few yards further and the tunnel was completely blocked with rock. There seemed to be little hope left.

"He's pinned under those rocks," Lizzie cried. "He may be dead. Mr Smithson's right."

Mr Brunel said nothing.

"Paddy's not dead," said Tom. "I'm going to find him."

Then Mr Brunel spoke. "Tom," he said. "I would never have thought to say such a thing as this, but now we are here in such straits, I must. No grown man would ever find his way over these piles of stone, but someone small might."

"Like me?" cried Tom.

"No!" said Lizzie. "It's too dangerous."

But before she could stop him he was clambering over the rocks and away from them.

"Listen," said Mr Brunel. Lizzie heard Tom's voice. He was singing "The Fields of Athenry".

★ ★ ★ ★

At first it seemed easy. But gradually, Tom began to wish he hadn't started this, as the rocks became more difficult. He had to keep hold of his candle somehow – but he needed both hands as well. In the end he stuck it in his mouth and felt his teeth biting into the unpleasant tasting tallow. This meant he could only hum "The Fields of Athenry".

But what was the point? There was no answer. He would soon have to go back –

if he could.

He was losing heart. Until – what was that? A faint sound. Someone very close was weakly singing "The Fields of Athenry". Tom dared to take the candle out of his mouth. "I've found him," he shouted.

* * * *

It was two hours later. Tom had found Paddy pinned down by stones but only

bruised. As soon as they heard Tom's shout, Mr Brunel sent Lizzie back to the spoil bucket with the message and soon navvies were coming down in numbers to move the rocks away. Tom stayed with Paddy until the way was clear and navvies could gently free him and carry him out. Then they and Mr Brunel walked back along the tunnel together and came to the surface again in the spoil bucket.

As they scrambled out, navvies formed into two ranks either side and clapped and cheered, and someone sang, "See the conquering heroes come."

"You and your sister are fine children," said Mr Brunel. "Tom, there'll be a place for you one day driving locomotives on the Great Western if you want to."

When Lizzie saw Tom's ecstatic face she knew that indeed his life's work was set out before him.

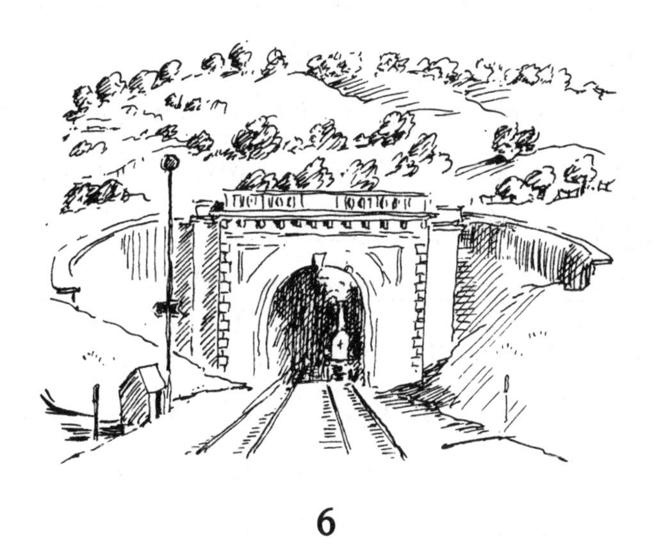

6

The railway comes at last

A year passed. In June 1841, the Box Tunnel, then the longest tunnel in the world, was finally finished and the railway was open all the way from Bristol to London.

It was a great day when the first train

came through. Everybody from the village was lining the embankment in their best clothes for such a memorable occasion. The rails gleamed in the sunshine. From far away came the new sound of a railway engine working hard. A plume of smoke and steam showed in the distance and drew nearer and nearer.

At last, it arrived, with a roar and a rush, a vision of huge wheels, a tall chimney, a copper dome standing on top of a long boiler, two men toiling with shovels, coal and fire, and a name – *North Star.*

Lizzie's pa said,
"Well, it's done. Didn't I
always say it would be?"
And Paddy smiled and said,
"Of course you did."

The coming of the railways

The beginnings

The first public railway in the world was the Stockton and Darlington Railway in the north-east of England, opened in 1825. The engineer was George Stephenson. In 1829, Stephenson and his son, Robert, won the Rainhill Trials – a competition to find the best engines for the new Liverpool and Manchester Railway – with their famous engine the "Rocket".

Soon railways were spreading across the land and the rest of the world. But when in 1834 the merchants of Bristol decided they needed a railway to London, it was not to George or Robert Stephenson that they turned, but to Isambard Kingdom Brunel.

Isambard Kingdom Brunel

Brunel was born in 1806. His father was a famous engineer, best known for building the Rotherhithe Tunnel, the first tunnel under the Thames. Isambard's first major work was in Bristol, designing the Clifton Suspension Bridge. Later he was asked to build the Great Western Railway. To help him round the country as he was building his railway, he designed his own black coach, as a mobile home and office. Everybody called it "the Flying Hearse".

When the railway was finished, Brunel turned to shipbuilding. The "Great Western", the "Great Britain" and finally the huge "Great Eastern" were the first steamships which were built like ships today. Paddington Station in London, the Saltash Bridge over the River Tamar and the old roof at Bristol Temple Meads Station, as well as bridges and tunnels on the railways to Bristol, Devon and Cornwall are all his work which you can still see today.

Would Brunel ever have gone down in the spoil bucket, as he does in this story? Yes, he certainly would – and often did. He was a man of great bravery – and expected others to be as well, often insisting the directors of the company came down with him. Like so many Victorian engineers, he was not afraid to think big and daringly put what he thought into practice.

THE GREAT EASTERN

Worn out with work, he died in 1858. So he never invented a source of steady and dependable light. This had to wait until 1879, when the American Thomas Edison invented the electric light bulb.

The Gauge Wars

When George Stephenson built his first railway he never thought of having any other distance between the rails (or "Gauge") than the width between the tracks on the old colliery tramways. This was four feet eight and a half inches (1.43 metres). Most railways built afterwards in Britain had the same gauge – except Brunel's. He could see no reason for using it just because it had always been used, so he invented the "Broad Gauge" which had seven feet (2.13 metres) between the rails. This meant his trains could be larger, more powerful and faster. However, Standard Gauge railways were cheaper to build and in the end the Broad Gauge lost the battle. Nearly every country in the world has railways with a gauge of four feet eight and a half inches.

BROAD GAUGE

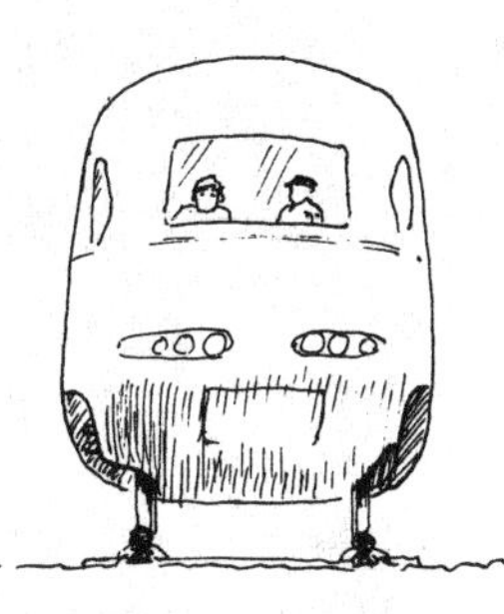

STANDARD GAUGE

Sparks: Historical Adventures

ANCIENT GREECE

The Great Horse of Troy – The Trojan War
0 7496 3369 7 (hbk) 0 7496 3538 X (pbk)
The Winner's Wreath – Ancient Greek Olympics
0 7496 3368 9 (hbk) 0 7496 3555 X (pbk)

INVADERS AND SETTLERS

Viking Raiders – A Norse Attack
0 7496 3089 2 (hbk) 0 7496 3457 X (pbk)
Boudica Strikes Back – The Romans in Britain
0 7496 3366 2 (hbk) 0 7496 3546 0 (pbk)
Erik's New Home – A Viking Town
0 7496 3367 0 (hbk) 0 7496 3552 5 (pbk)

TALES OF THE ROWDY ROMANS

The Great Necklace Hunt
0 7496 2221 0 (hbk) 0 7496 2628 3 (pbk)
The Lost Legionary
0 7496 2222 9 (hbk) 0 7496 2629 1 (pbk)
The Guard Dog Geese
0 7496 2331 4 (hbk) 0 7496 2630 5 (pbk)
A Runaway Donkey
0 7496 2332 2 (hbk) 0 7496 2631 3 (pbk)

TUDORS AND STUARTS

Captain Drake's Orders – The Armada
0 7496 2556 2 (hbk) 0 7496 3121 X (pbk)
London's Burning – The Great Fire of London
0 7496 2557 0 (hbk) 0 7496 3122 8 (pbk)
Mystery at the Globe – Shakespeare's Theatre
0 7496 3096 5 (hbk) 0 7496 3449 9 (pbk)
Stranger in the Glen – Rob Roy
0 7496 2586 4 (hbk) 0 7496 3123 6 (pbk)
A Dream of Danger – The Massacre of Glencoe
0 7496 2587 2 (hbk) 0 7496 3124 4 (pbk)
A Queen's Promise – Mary Queen of Scots
0 7496 2589 9 (hbk) 0 7496 3125 2 (pbk)
Over the Sea to Skye – Bonnie Prince Charlie
0 7496 2588 0 (hbk) 0 7496 3126 0 (pbk)
Plague! – A Tudor Epidemic
0 7496 3365 4 (hbk) 0 7496 3556 8 (pbk)

TALES OF A TUDOR TEARAWAY

A Pig Called Henry
0 7496 2204 4 (hbk) 0 7496 2625 9 (pbk)
A Horse Called Deathblow
0 7496 2205 9 (hbk) 0 7496 2624 0 (pbk)
Dancing for Captain Drake
0 7496 2234 2 (hbk) 0 7496 2626 7 (pbk)
Birthdays are a Serious Business
0 7496 2235 0 (hbk) 0 7496 2627 5 (pbk)

VICTORIAN ERA

The Runaway Slave – The British Slave Trade
0 7496 3093 0 (hbk) 0 7496 3456 1 (pbk)
The Sewer Sleuth – Victorian Cholera
0 7496 2590 2 (hbk) 0 7496 3128 7 (pbk)
Convict! – Criminals Sent to Australia
0 7496 2591 0 (hbk) 0 7496 3129 5 (pbk)
The Great Raj – The British in India
0 7496 3090 6 (hbk) 0 7496 3451 0 (pbk)
Farewell to Ireland – Emigration to America
0 7496 3094 9 (hbk) 0 7496 3448 0 (pbk)
The Great Hunger – Famine in Ireland
0 7496 3095 7 (hbk) 0 7496 3447 2 (pbk)
Fire Down the Pit – A Welsh Mining Disaster
0 7496 3091 4 (hbk) 0 7496 3450 2 (pbk)
Tunnel Rescue – The Great Western Railway
0 7496 3353 0 (hbk) 0 7496 3537 1 (pbk)
Kidnap on the Canal – Victorian Waterways
0 7496 3352 2 (hbk) 0 7496 3540 1 (pbk)
Dr. Barnardo's Boys – Victorian Charity
0 7496 3358 1 (hbk) 0 7496 3541 X (pbk)
The Iron Ship – Brunel's Great Britain
0 7496 3355 7 (hbk) 0 7496 3543 6 (pbk)
Bodies for Sale – Victorian Tomb-Robbers
0 7496 3364 6 (hbk) 0 7496 3539 8 (pbk)
Penny Post Boy – The Victorian Postal Service
0 7496 3362 X (hbk) 0 7496 3544 4 (pbk)
The Canal Diggers – The Manchester Ship Canal
0 7496 3356 5 (hbk) 0 7496 3545 2 (pbk)
The Tay Bridge Tragedy – A Victorian Disaster
0 7496 3354 9 (hbk) 0 7496 3547 9 (pbk)
Stop, Thief! – The Victorian Police
0 7496 3359 X (hbk) 0 7496 3548 7 (pbk)
Miss Buss and Miss Beale – Victorian Schools
0 7496 3360 3 (hbk) 0 7496 3549 5 (pbk)
Chimney Charlie – Victorian Chimney Sweeps
0 7496 3351 4 (hbk) 0 7496 3551 7 (pbk)
Down the Drain – Victorian Sewers
0 7496 3357 3 (hbk) 0 7496 3550 9 (pbk)
The Ideal Home – A Victorian New Town
0 7496 3361 1 (hbk) 0 7496 3553 3 (pbk)
Stage Struck – Victorian Music Hall
0 7496 3367 0 (hbk) 0 7496 3554 1 (pbk)

TRAVELS OF A YOUNG VICTORIAN

The Golden Key
0 7496 2360 8 (hbk) 0 7496 2632 1 (pbk)
Poppy's Big Push
0 7496 2361 6 (hbk) 0 7496 2633 X (pbk)
Poppy's Secret
0 7496 2374 8 (hbk) 0 7496 2634 8 (pbk)
The Lost Treasure
0 7496 2375 6 (hbk) 0 7496 2635 6 (pbk)

20th-CENTURY HISTORY

Fight for the Vote – The Suffragettes
0 7496 3092 2 (hbk) 0 7496 3452 9 (pbk)
The Road to London – The Jarrow March
0 7496 2609 7 (hbk) 0 7496 3132 5 (pbk)
The Sandbag Secret – The Blitz
0 7496 2608 9 (hbk) 0 7496 3133 3 (pbk)
Sid's War – Evacuation
0 7496 3209 7 (hbk) 0 7496 3445 6 (pbk)
D-Day! – Wartime Adventure
0 7496 3208 9 (hbk) 0 7496 3446 4 (pbk)
The Prisoner – A Prisoner of War
0 7496 3212 7 (hbk) 0 7496 3455 3 (pbk)
Escape from Germany – Wartime Refugees
0 7496 3211 9 (hbk) 0 7496 3454 5 (pbk)
Flying Bombs – Wartime Bomb Disposal
0 7496 3210 0 (hbk) 0 7496 3453 7 (pbk)
12,000 Miles From Home – Sent to Australia
0 7496 3370 0 (hbk) 0 7496 3542 8 (pbk)